Learning Points

- Children love finding out about the jobs that other people do and they are especially interested by the people whose jobs help them – such as shopkeepers, postal workers and nurses.
  It's exciting for children to recognise and learn more about them in their own books.

- Have fun talking about all the interesting details in the pictures and encourage children to talk about their own experiences. What are their teachers like? Have they ever seen a builder at work or visited the hairdressers?

Ladybird books are widely available, but in case of difficulty may be ordered by post or telephone from:

Ladybird Books – Cash Sales Department
Littlegate Road Paignton Devon TQ3 3BE
Telephone 01803 554761

A catalogue record for this book is available
from the British Library

Published by Ladybird Books Ltd Loughborough Leicestershire UK
Ladybird Books Inc Auburn Maine 04210 USA

let's look at
People
At Work

by Karen Bryant-Mole

illustrated by Norman Young

Ladybird

Shopkeepers

Shopkeepers sell things such as food, clothes and books.

Mr Ashington is filling up
shelves in his shop.
What is happening to the
pile of tins?

Builders

Chris is helping to build new houses on this building site. He is using a wheelbarrow to move some concrete.

Can you find Chris? What else
can you see in the picture?

Car Mechanics

Car mechanics look after cars and fix them when they go wrong. Nicky is mending a puncture.

Can you see what the other
mechanics are doing?

Vets

Vets care for animals. Jamie has brought his cat, Tiger, to the vet. Tiger has hurt his paw.

Who else is waiting to see the vet? Do you think the little girl will catch her rabbit?

Factory Workers

Factory workers help to make things. Each worker has a special job to do.

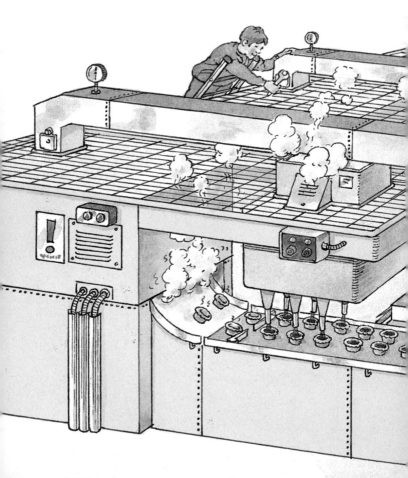

Joyce works in a cake factory.
She packs little cakes in boxes.
Can you see her?

Nurses

Nurses look after sick people in hospitals.

Steven is a nurse, he is taking
Lucy's temperature.
Can you see Lucy's teddy?

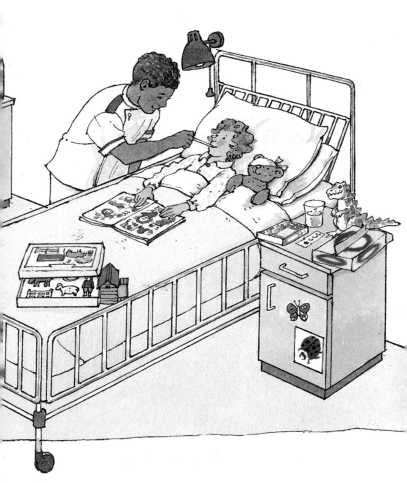

Dentists

Dentists look after our teeth and teach us how to brush them properly. Matt is having a check-up.

Mrs Reid can see that Matt has been brushing his teeth well.
Do you brush your teeth well?

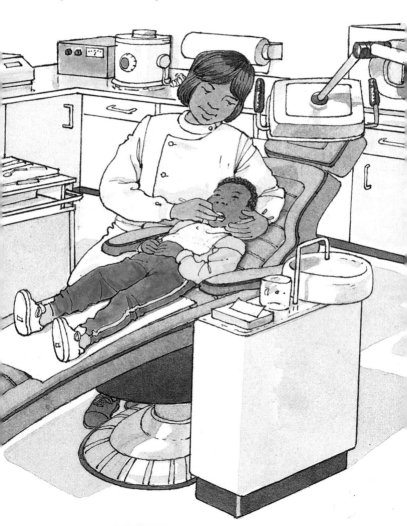

Farmers

Farmers start work early in the morning. Pete has brought his cows to be milked. He is shutting the gate behind them.

The milk lorry is waiting to
collect all the fresh milk.
Do you like milk?

Plumbers

Plumbers put baths, sinks, showers and radiators in houses. They mend leaks too.

Mr Singh has nearly finished
putting a new sink in this
bathroom. Kate can't wait
to use it!

Teachers

Most teachers teach children in schools. There are lots of exciting things to learn in the classroom.

Miss Elliot is teaching Class 3b a new song. What kind of instruments are the children playing?

Postal Workers

Postal workers sort the post and deliver it to the right houses. Ruby is bringing cards and parcels to this house.

The little boy is really excited.
Do you think it is his birthday?

Hairdressers

Hairdressers cut hair. They wash and curl hair too. Jane is cutting Sarah's hair. The little bits of hair are tickling Sarah's neck.

Do you wriggle when you have
your hair cut?
Can you see the lady under
the hairdryer?

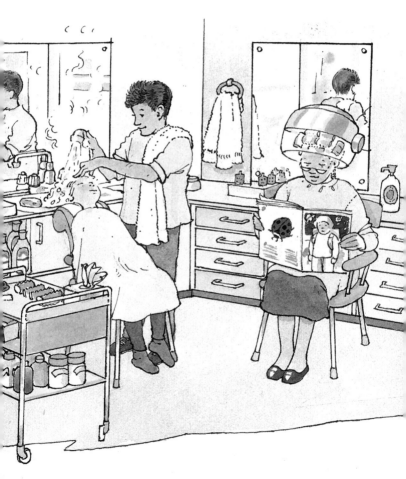